Collected

Thomas LaSalle

"This collection of short stories is dedicated to my wonderful fiancée, who has always believed in me, and to my wonderful family."

ISBN: 978-0-557-92302-1

Table of Contents

Introduction

Writing, any way you wish to look at it, is almost certainly a form of art. I'm well aware that everybody has their favorite painting or photograph. To me, art is defined as a piece that expresses great creativity and/or provokes thought. By those standards, certainly we could consider writing to be a form of art. Some of the greatest stories of all time have led us to think. They have led us to wonder. Many stories leave us on the edge of our seats, keeping us wondering what is to come. Yet, there are other stories that resolve themselves prior to the end.

I, by no stretch of the imagination, are a professional writer. I am a young college student, a student of the arts. I am following one of my greatest passions, writing. My aim is to entertain, to explore the absurd, the surreal, and anything else that can provoke thought in people from all walks of life. I aim to provoke thought in people ranging from the youngest, most novice readers, to the professionals who analyze every minute detail of every paragraph, every word. My goal, above all, is to entertain.

This may seem like a very unusual goal for a writer, but by my experience it seems to be the end result for many well written pieces by highly regarded professionals. I hold many writers in such high regard, and try to read as many pieces as I can. I try to find inspiration in the littlest things, I look for it everywhere. The end result is this collection of short stories I have to present to you. Some of them were written for school projects. Others were written purely for my own amusement. And yet, others were written for the entertainment of my closest friends and relatives. And yet, I have chosen to present them to you, some in a fairly raw form, yet mostly polished for your enjoyment.

Writing is almost certainly an art, and a popular one at that. If you are an avid reader and have yet to write a masterpiece of your own, I greatly implore you to. After all, the next big thing almost certainly starts off as something small, before it grows into something to be beloved by the world. You may very well come up with the next big thing.

Happy Reading!

Great Joy

Joy was a simple girl, though anyone who knew her for her entire life would be shocked at how she had changed. She spent her days working as a Veterinarian's Assistant for her local animal hospital, and at night, she took classes in nursing. It was helping animals that brought her the most elation. It all stemmed from the age of 10, when she found an injured puppy on the side of the road. Her school was only a block away from her house in Suburban Chicago, so her mother felt comfortable letting her walk home with her friends. It was one rainy April afternoon on one of those walks home when Joy saw him, lying in the road, whimpering weakly. One of his hind legs was contorted in a position which it should not have been, and a look of melancholy was spread across his face. Joy picked him up, tenderly, and ran home, sheltering the injured puppy from the rain. She ran into the house as fast as she could, the small dog whimpering, as if he were sobbing profusely. Joy ran up to her mother, a middle aged woman, short in stature but with a big heart.

"Mommy!" shouted Joy, "This poor puppy! He's hurt!"

"Is he?" said her mother with a sense of compassion, "Let me see him."

Joy handed over the puppy to her mother, who took him softly in her arms. The puppy whimpered slightly as he looked at the mother with wistful eyes, filled with such hurt and sadness, one would suspect cruelty; however the puppy did not come with a collar or a tag, so they couldn't tell who the owner was. The mother set the puppy on a cushion and examined the leg thoroughly. She touched at it gingerly, as to not cause any more discomfort. She lifted the puppy in her arms.

"We need to get him to a vet, right away," said the mother, "I think his leg might be broken."

And for the first time in her life past infancy, Joy shed a tear. She had been afraid to cry because of her father. Her father, a drunk, would beat her on a nightly basis after a long night at the bar. He had warned her never to cry, or he would come at her harder. Harder, and quicker, and Joy was afraid of him already. And about a year ago, he passed away from liver failure. And though he was out of her life at that moment, the scars were permanent. Joy remained as emotionless as a stone alongside the river. She was afraid of emotion, mostly of the "consequences" of emotion. She did not want to face anybody's wrath, let alone bring it on by crying, and yet here she was, shedding a tear for an injured puppy that she had never known before. And yet, nothing was happening to her.

Joy and her mother hopped into their minivan, Joy cradling the puppy in her arms. Joy looked down at the puppy, whose whimper began to get weaker, slowly. Despite that, the puppy began to wag its tail, enjoying the attention from Joy. Joy choked back another tear as her mother pulled out of the driveway and turned down a side street, going as fast as she could while trying to stay within the legal limits. They drove past a pet store on the main street. Joy caught a glimpse through the store window. There were several puppies of different sizes and colors, all of them playing excitedly with each other. It was at that moment that Joy smiled, which was a much different look from the "stone face" that she had worn daily.

It was only a short while later before they arrived at the animal hospital. It was a small, grey building, with carvings of different pets on different points on the building. Across the street from the hospital is a cemetery, the same cemetery where Joy's father was supposed to be buried. Joy's mother decided to stop keeping track of him once Joy was 6, though the damage had already been done by then. They entered the building, which was empty except for a receptionist and a couple of nurses.

"I'm going to check us in," said Joy's mother, "you take the puppy and have a seat over there."

Joy nodded her head and sat down in a chair while her mother talked to the receptionist, a sort of panicked expression on her face. Joy looked down at the puppy, who continued to whimper. She smiled as she pet the puppy on its head and began to scratch behind its ears. The puppy put on a slight smile as it wagged its tail harder. Joy laughed as she continued to scratch the puppy behind its ears, another thing she had lacked in her life was laughter, yet it seemed like nothing could keep her from it now. Soon enough, Joy's mother called her over and they went into the back, where the exam rooms were. Joy set the puppy down on the padded table and went to sit down next to her mother. The puppy watched Joy with attentive eyes and attempted to run after her, but to no avail. His eyes began to fill with sadness as Joy watched it, smiling.

"I have never seen you quite like this," said Joy's mother.

"That poor puppy, but he's so cute," said Joy, "I hope the doctor can fix him."

"I'm sure he can," said Joy's mother, "this is the best animal hospital in town. I think your puppy will be just fine."

Joy's mothers' eyes began to well up as she watched her daughter smile and giggle. It had been such a long time since Joy had smiled like that. Joy's days would usually have her come home, do her homework, eat dinner, and go to bed. She never went out to play with the other children; she had never even noticed other children. And she certainly never took this sort of interest in animals. Usually, when the neighbors would go out and walk their dogs, Joy would point and say "Eww, mommy, those are gross," in a very monotonous voice. Her mother would oftentimes worry about her, going so far as to speak to a psychiatrist about her. She would take weekly visits to therapy, just to continue holding in her emotions, for fear that the psychiatrist would beat her.

But now, she was doing things her mother would call "very un-Joy like, yet very en-Joy-able." She was smiling, crying and laughing.

Most importantly, she was showing recognition and a sense of urgency and caring for another life. Within a moment's notice, the vet walked in, tall and handsome in a white overcoat. He inspected the puppy thoroughly, taking his temperature, checking his weight, and giving him his shots. He motioned for Joy to leave the room, and she did. She knew the vet had to do something to the puppy to make him well again that she might not be comfortable seeing. After a loud whimper emerged from the back, the vet and Joy's mother emerged from the back, smiling.

"Your puppy is going to be just fine," said the vet, "his leg was dislocated and we were able to set it back in place. I will prescribe him some medicine, but after a week he should be just fine."

Joy squealed with excitement and ran towards her mother, throwing her arms around her in a tight squeeze. Her mother began to cry. Not only was she happy for the puppy, but she was happy for her daughter. After all these years, finally, Joy was free.

Over time, Joy continued to grow, not only physically, but emotionally as well. Her mother watched in great delight, as over the years she began to become more social, more open to friendships. She graduated at the top of her High School class, giving a speech at graduation about how she had evolved as a person, thanks to the one day at the veterinarian's office, her mother choking back tears of joy.

One night, after nursing classes had let out, Joy drove to her apartment downtown. She ascended the stairs, unlocked her door and opened it. Before she could even set foot inside, a chocolate lab tackled her, sending her flying backwards into the hallway and onto the hallway floor. She laughed as the lab licked her face.

"Baxter, stop, I'm happy to see you too," she giggled as she lifted the big dog off of her. Baxter, the hurt puppy that Joy found on the side of the road, was now one of Joy's best friends, and just how Baxter had grown up, so had Joy. Only this time, there was no reason for fear.

Empty Nest

The children have left. My twin boys have gone off to college. New York University, both of them. Both on the same day, both at the same time, and both for the same thing. For about the first week or so, my wife and I lived our lives as normal. I would go off to my job at the Daily Chronicle every morning at 9, kissing my wife goodbye as I walked out the back door. She would stay around the house, partaking in the cooking, the cleaning and the shopping. I would work a full day's shift, and walk back through our back door again at 5 that night, kissing my wife hello. We would sit and eat, joking around, discussing current events. It seemed as if nothing were different at all.

It would not be until as recently as yesterday that my wife and I would walk past the boy's old room. Being the brave soul that I am, I decided to take a step inside. All that remained were two beds, a chest of drawers, and an old wooden toy box. I walked up to that toy box and opened it up, peering inside. On the inside was a cavalcade of old toys and games. I reached inside and pulled out Billy's old roller skates. It was at that very moment that it hit me like a ton of bricks. The emptiness of the room, the sight of their old toys, it occurred to me that things were a lot more different than they seemed.

To be honest, I had feared this day for the longest time. I am not one who enjoys an empty house, and for the last week or two I deluded myself into the fantasy that nothing had changed. I had made myself believe that nothing was different, yet I had always been afraid of reality setting in. This was possibly due to me knowing about the inevitable. My boys grew up enjoying the same activities. They shared just about everything that they owned. They even shared a room up until they left, and they may possibly even be sharing a room now. My wife and I were certainly grateful, in that we didn't have to buy double the amount of toys.

But then, they say that boys will be boys, and our boys were no exception. They were always getting into trouble in school, picking fights on the playground, and finding snails in the wooded area behind our house and bringing them home, hiding them in their pockets in hopes we wouldn't notice. We somehow always knew they were bringing things into our house that didn't belong. One time, when Billy was about 8, found a snake in that wooded area. He brought it into the house with him, and it somehow found its way from his room into our bed. My wife certainly got quite the scare when she found it.

Yet, our boys were also pretty responsible. They knew when to do the right thing when the situation presented itself. There was one day, when Robbie was 9 or 10, he found an envelope on the side of the road on his way home from school. He brought it to my wife as soon as he got home, and she held on to it until I got home. She showed me the envelope, which contained about a few hundred dollars, and a golden necklace. That was certainly something one would not like to lose on the side of the road. My wife inquired of me, "Would you take this to the police station? Robbie wanted to know, he's not sure where it is." That brought a smile to my face. Although my boys had been through a lot of mischief, it felt good to know that I raised them right.

I placed the old roller skates back into the old toy box and shut the lid. I looked out the window at the woods behind the house. I'm sure it was definitely my mind playing tricks on me, but I could swear that I saw Billy walk from the woods with a green snake in his hands, and I could swear that I saw young Robbie walk from the woods holding an envelope with a few hundred dollars in his hands. I ran down the stairs to the back door, expecting two young boys to come walking through.

Nobody came.

My wife put her hands on my shoulders and gave them a rub. She knew how I felt, and she sympathized. I never wanted this day to come, but it had to. Things were certainly never going to be the same.

Edison

They say he's close. They say he's close to completing his latest invention. He's close to creating a means of lighting up a room using electricity. It all started with some silly little experiments. He'd run around outside, flying a kite in stormy weather. It seemed like the poor sap was looking for a way to kill himself. Nobody was truly aware of what he really wanted to do. Before anybody knew it, he was the talk of the town. All these silly little experiments caught everybody's attention.

I, too, am an inventor. Many people have told me that I'm mad. Many other people have told me that I'm just jealous, that I'd never be able to stand up to him. I'd invent something that I thought would be useful, no, that I knew would be useful. I'd invent things that I thought would benefit the everyday lives of humankind. I had ideas; ideas of building a device that would record sound and play it back. It was going to be golden, pure genius. But when I went to present my idea to the citizens of Menlo Park, there he was, demonstrating a completed device; a device which could record sounds and plays it back.

There I was, a complete fool. If I would have told anybody that it was my idea, they would have shrugged me off. They would have told me that I was crazy, they always did. However, I was not the crazy one. How many weird, crazy experiments did it take him to come up with a device that I'm positive needed none. They might be correct; I might be just a tad insane. I might be just a wee bit crazy, but I'm brilliant, and isn't it the insanity that fosters brilliance?

He began to become the hero of the town. The mayor considered changing the name of the town, so that it was named after him. All I could do was stand back and watch, as my ideas went to shame as he found his fifteen minutes of fame. I was labeled as nothing but a sham, an outcast, if you will. It is something that I could certainly never be proud of in my entire existence. I had never planned on becoming the town's fool.

But now, I've got a different plan; a completely different idea that will hopefully bring me the respect that I deserve and the adoration of the people living in this Podunk town. And then, maybe the ridicule will finally end. Maybe my foolish feelings will finally come to a close. I have not told anybody else about what I plan to do. Surely, if I were to share my latest and greatest idea with somebody else, they would definitely commit me to some institution of sorts. A place where they would have close yet careful surveillance on me day after day. A place where I would be forced into straightjackets, have pills shoved down my throat…

Instead, I have decided to entrust my plan to only myself, but in you as well, because I'm sure that I can trust you. I walk into my study, and push aside the tallest bookshelf. Behind is my antique musket. I have not laid a finger on that thing since it was passed on to me by my father, who in turn had not touched it since it was passed on to him by his father, and so forth. My great, great grandfather was a hero in the American Revolution, and my father had told me that the gun had belonged to him. Fancy that, I was about to fulfill my own heroic deed with such a heroic musket.

It is nearly seven in the evening as I slink my way outside his window. I creak up to his front door and slowly open it. And there it is, on his workbench. I slowly creep over and pick it off the table. It is a glass globe with copper wiring inside of it. Is this his greatest invention yet? How would this paltry glass globe benefit mankind? How could something so simple be considered the greatest thing? This stupid thing is supposed to light up a room. Even though something like this would make him seem so moronic, I could not let him present this abomination to the town.

I slowly creep over to his bed and glance at him, asleep. I watch as his chest rises and falls, rises and falls. I can bear to watch this no longer. I hold the musket, pointed straight for his temple. Without any thought, I pull the trigger. A loud scream emerges from his mouth as it contorts into a weird shape. Within seconds, he falls back to the mattress, limp, blood pouring from the hole in front of his head. I stand above his lifeless body, not sure what to expect.

I knew the people of this town would eventually discover him here, dead. I knew they would eventually trace this back to me. In the distance, I heard a small commotion. Doors creaked open, footsteps began to inch closer. The town had heard the gunshot, and they were surely coming to check on him; coming to see if they could catch his killer in the act. I knew exactly what I had to do.

I swiftly ran through his house toward a back window. As quickly as I could, I flung the window open, off its hinges, and dove through, musket and all. In the distance, I could see the faint lights of candles and torches, and the continuous marching of boots crunching along the dirt path. I removed my shoes as to lighten the noise, and sprang into a gallop, running as fast as my legs could carry me toward the woods behind his house.

I darted amongst the trees, being careful not to make too much noise. It would only be a matter of minutes before they would arrive at his house, discover him dead, and then discover the killer had sprung through a back window and escaped into the woods. These very woods which seemed to extend forever. If there was supposed to be a way out, it had certainly avoided my grasp. I darted left and right, only aided by the light of the full moon. It wasn't long before the sounds of footsteps and the sight of torches had faded away, and I stopped, out of breath.

I had done the world a great justice, of which the likes of mankind had never seen. Never again would I feel the torture of being second best to the craziest man in town. Never again would I have to live in his shadow. Yet at the same time, I would never again be able to live amongst civilization. I would always be deemed a killer, an insane killer.

Yet, I am also a brilliant killer, because insanity surely does foster brilliance.

~*~

What I had assumed was a week had passed by, though it might have been more. I had taken refuge in a cavern a distance outside of Menlo Park. Word of his passing had spread like wildfire, yet nobody knew who had killed him, they only knew of his escape. Not one person was willing to work on any of his prototypes, as they were either too nervous or not brilliant enough. What had made me curious was why nobody had bothered to search for me. Surely, if somebody had slain their great hero, they would want to know who.

Day after day, these thoughts clouded my mind, and haunted my soul. I could not find the strength to eat, sleep or do anything at all. What was wrong with me? Why was I feeling tortured over these people not caring about who had killed him. I felt like I had accomplished a great deed, yet at the same time I also feel like I've accomplished nothing. Like he had done many times before, I had benefitted mankind, yet I had not gotten one ounce of recognition or glory for it. I wanted to be heralded for what I'd done, I wanted to be recognized, and I wanted my time in the sun. I knew what had to be done.

The sun rose the next day, burning my sleepless eyes with its fury. As with every other night, I had gotten no sleep. This time, however, was different, as I was planning on what I would say or do when I returned. Nothing had come to mind immediately, which led me to believe that I should improvise.

I began to walk back to Menlo Park, musket in hand. The soft grass started tickling my bare feet with every step that I took. A few blue songbirds flew by, whistling their happy tune. The only thing I could think about was getting my recognition. I strolled along at an exhausted pace, winding my way through the trees as I had on the fateful night. My legs felt like rubber and my eyelids felt like they had weights tied to them. I had to keep going, however, for I wanted my deed to remain fresh in everybody's mind.

It wasn't long before I finally arrived in Menlo Park. I could not believe the sight. Just about every citizen of the town was in black and in a somber mood as well. Nobody bothered to look up, either; they just kept their heads down and continued their silent death march. What had happened here? I expected everybody to look to me as a hero, yet nobody looked to me at all. One person looked up at me, saw the musket in my hand as well as my blood stained clothes, and uttered a sick gasp. This, in turn, caused the rest of the people to look up at me in unison.

A wide smile spread across my face, for I knew my moment of recognition was at hand. Rather than faces of celebration, however, all I saw were faces of disgust, faces of anger, and faces of betrayal. One woman in the crowd started sobbing. Almost immediately, they began to inch closer to me, their faces getting angrier. Could this be why I felt the way I did this entire time. Could it be that I was not proud of what I had done. Surely, it couldn't be, I was supposed to be proud. I was supposed to be celebrated. The people inched closer, there was to be no celebration today. I knew what I had to do.

I put the musket to my head and pulled the trig…

Depression

I stand here in line, watching, and waiting. It feels like this line stretches on for miles and miles, though in reality the market is only in the middle of the block. It is extremely cold out here, and the ground is covered in a fresh blanket of snow. The line that I am standing in seems to be moving as slowly as possible, as if to taunt me. I stand here, continuing to remind myself "it's only a bread line," though it feels like the line of death.

I read the newspaper with my breakfast this morning, as I usually do every morning. They say that this should all be over soon. They say that the economy should rebound. They say that people should soon be able to find decent jobs. President Roosevelt continues to tell the people of this fine nation that he is working around the clock, working to find a solution. There is nothing better for me to do with my time besides read the paper, and wait in line for bread. I lost my job about two months ago, and ever since then I had to learn to become accustomed to bread lines and newspapers, and plain old not working. I'd love to get back to work, and make a difference in the lives of myself and others, but it feels as if President Roosevelt is taking his sweet time creating results for the American people.

And so, I usually spend every Wednesday waiting in this line, in any kind of extreme weather. There are usually so many familiar faces. As if it were meant to be, I usually always wait behind a young mother of about 21, wrapped in a shawl, holding her infant son tight in her arms. Hopefully by the time the infant is her age, he won't have to experience the torment of bread lines. Waiting behind me is the same old man, maybe 60 at the least, in a dark brown overcoat and loafers. He usually attempts to talk my ear off, though I try not to listen. However, it is hard for me to help myself, because the old man can at times be wise beyond his years. He is a veteran of the first World War, so most of his discussions involve his time as an Army commander.

Yet he also makes valiant attempts to predict the future. "Roosevelt may make things better, but it won't last long," he'd say in a shaky voice, "future generations will see the same turmoil. I'm ashamed to say it, but I'd be damned if it wasn't the truth." A lot of his rants would scare me; they would send shivers down my spine worse than the cold air would. Yet, I could not help but listen to the stories and the predictions for a future as bad as the present that we were experiencing. Something about the way he spoke told me that he was serious, yet at the same time the shock I experienced led me to believe that it was all true.

Yet on this day, the old man was not in line behind me. Instead, it was his son, who had notified me that the old man suffered a heart attack the previous night, and passed away en route to the hospital. A sad story indeed, and hearing about it did not help my plight in the least. As I waited in the line, I looked across the street at two young boys. They could not have been older than six years old. I watched as they had a merry little snowball fight, laughing gaily with each toss of a snowball. I'm not sure why, but something about that scene brought a smile to my face that day. They called that period that we were going through a "great depression." However, watching the boys have a grand old time in the snow gave me new hope. These boys were not depressed in the least. They did not even seem to be effected by anything going on around them. They ignored the line of frozen people across the street, waiting for rations, and threw snowballs at each other.

That scene made me think about everything, about the news articles, about the president and the bread line and the old man and his stories, and really take it into perspective. They call this time period "The great depression," but that doesn't mean we really have to be depressed. If we ever come out of it as the president says, or if we ever go back into it as the old man said, is one thing, but I found newfound strength that day to stand in that bread line with a wide grin on my face on the coldest of days.

Death

My grandfather had reached the end of his rope. The cancer had spread throughout his body and was as close to his brain as a devoted Christian is close to his savior. The doctor, in as dreary a tone as we could bear, told us "one week." None of us wanted to believe it, but we knew the inevitable was finally here. And even though my grandfather knew it as well, he was a lot more cheery than anybody in my family put together. He knew he lived a good life, a fulfilling life, and he knew that if he was going to go out, he was going to go with a smile on his face. After all, he was always known for that smile.

Though, they say almost every man has his regrets, and that amends should probably be made before passing on. One day, I visited my grandfather with my father, his son-in-law, maybe about a day before the doctor had stated that he would meet his maker. My grandfather was in the best of spirits, as always, which honestly began to make me feel a whole lot brighter. My father, however, was not fazed by my grandfather's cheerfulness. My grandfather and my father did not like each other at all, ever since the day my father went on the first date with my mother. Something about my father rubbed my grandfather the wrong way, and it had been that way until now. Though my father was reluctant to come along, my mother had been by to see grandpa earlier in the day, and had errands to run later on. Since I couldn't go by myself, I had to go with my father.

And now, we stood in the hospital room. I ran up to my grandfather and gave him the biggest hug ever, almost like I had never seen him my entire life, and was just meeting him for the very first time. He hugged me back tightly and gave me a pat on the head.

"I'm so glad you could come today, I got worried when you weren't with your mother," he said with his usual warm smile.

“I had to go to school today, grandpa,” I replied, “I couldn’t come until now.”

“Ah,” he exclaimed, teeming with excitement. My grandfather had always wanted me to succeed, and he knew a good education was a good start.

“Why don’t you go into the waiting area for a few seconds,” he said, “I have to talk to your father about something.” I nodded my head and skipped out the door and into the waiting area. Being the nosy young boy that I was, I stood outside the door to listen in to their conversation.

“David, there is something I’ve been wanting to tell you,” my grandfather said, his voice changing from that of an excited old man to a more serious tone.

“Whatever it is, let’s just get it over with quickly,” my father said sheepishly. He was used to my grandfather not liking him, and although he didn’t want it to be that way, he knew that there was nothing that he could do about it. There was, however, something my grandfather could do about it, and I assume in times like these, these kind of things come a little easier.

“My life,” grandpa started, pausing for a second to think before continuing, “my life hasn’t been as exciting as I made others believe.” My father just stood there, silent, expecting something semi-insulting to emerge from the dying man’s lips, but he did not expect what was coming next.

“Son,” he started, which caught my father by absolute surprise. Never in a million years would my grandfather call my father “son.” It just did not happen. “I was hoping it wouldn’t take me ‘til I was on my deathbed to realize this, but I was always a foolish old nut. I always said I cared about my daughter’s happiness, but I’ve never respected the one part of her life that made her truly happy.”

My father was taken aback by these words. Were they really coming from my grandfather? What he said next was really shocking.

"I changed my mind about you, you really are a great guy, and I must say I'm proud to call you my son." My grandfather never had any boys. My mother has two sisters, but never any brothers. My father was the closest thing to a son that my grandfather ever had, and until now had pushed him away almost completely. As my father stood there, my grandfather held out his hand, motioning for my father to hold it. My father took a nervous step backwards before, almost as if there was a magnetic force drawing him closer, he moved in to hold my grandfather's hand. A single tear graced my eye. I was aware of the distance between the two men, but for one shining moment, they were one.

~*~

My grandfather passed away the next morning, and for once my father cried. Never in a million years would I ever have expected my father to cry for my grandfather. Yet, he cried almost like he was a child who had lost his father. In a way, that morning, he really had lost his father.

Hollywood Hotshot

You need money, and a lot of it, first and foremost. Nobody makes it in Hollywood without money. You start by washing cars for fifty cents apiece. Your mom rewards a hard day's work with lemonade and cookies. Munch down your cookies and drink your lemonade and get back to work, because these cars don't wash themselves. After you count your day's earnings, you see you've made ten dollars, and you realize you're on the right track. You should also do odd jobs for some of your parent's friends. Mrs. Paulson asks you to walk her ten dogs. You want to tell her that she's crazy, but you do it anyway. The dogs are feisty and are certainly more excited about this walk than you are. Three of the dogs are stricken with poor bowel control. Hold back your need to throw up as you clean up after them. Bring the dogs home and Mrs. Paulson hands you a crisp twenty. Check the validity of the twenty, shake her hand, and run out her door, vowing never to return.

Once you reach High School, join the theater club. Take some acting classes at the local community center. Any experience you can get can be useful in the long run. Audition for the school's production of Romeo and Juliet, and not get cast. You need to experience rejection if you ever hope to make it in Hollywood. Don't shake the director's hand, as this can be shown as a sign of "raising the white flag." Find a job at a fast food joint in your continued attempt to save money. Flip the burgers every two minutes, being cautious not to drop any on the floor. You get a little too excited and accidently drop a burger on the floor. Throw it away, don't be like John Washington, who decided it was ok to serve it to a customer. The lawsuits forced the old owners to sell the place.

After about a year, you should have approximately one-thousand two-hundred and forty-two dollars saved up. Unfortunately, you are let go from your job after another "floor-burger" incident forces the state to shut down the restaurant. Take the money you have saved and invest it in a good savings account. Try for one that pays more than one percent interest, which in this day and age is almost impossible. When you open the savings account, make sure to comment on how nice the branch manager looks today. She will look at you with that weird look as to ask "are you kissing up to me for a reason?" Try to let it go and don't forget to sign everywhere you are told to sign. About a week after you open the account, you notice that ten dollars went missing. Because you forgot to read the fine print, you got hit with the ten dollar a month service charge for not having the two-thousand dollar minimum balance in your account. Proceed to kick yourself for this.

Continue to audition for school plays and plays at the community center. You finally land a role as Hamlet in the community center's production. You receive a copy of the script and are asked to come back in a week for the first rehearsal. Study your lines hard. Make sure you know how every single word is pronounced, and make sure you are spelling it right. Grab the script from out of Rover's mouth, before it becomes his lunch. Ask the director for another script once you realize that it's too late. At your first week of rehearsal, you begin by rehearsing the second scene in the play. You start to feel stage fright and ask for a glass of water. Gulp it down, and try to remember your lines as best as you can. As you say your lines, you realize that you have trouble reciting old English, and stumble on words as simple as "thee" and as complex as "satyr." You are booted from the cast, the director wondering what she ever saw in you in the first place. Just shrug your shoulders, and walk home, running from a vicious pit bull that has gotten loose.

After you have saved up at least five-thousand dollars by working various jobs and somehow being suckered into walking Mrs. Paulson's dogs again, you will need to move to California. Buy your ticket, and make sure it is first-class. If you want to live like a hot shot, there is no better time to start than on the plane. Hail a cab, and make sure the driver's name is Amir. You've known at least two Amir's in your lifetime, and they have both been upstanding, funny people and good friends. After you hop in the taxi, you realize that the driver's name is Rashid. Smack yourself in the forehead for not succeeding in your mission. Arrive at the airport two hours early, because you may spend at least an hour and fifty-five minutes getting through security. Once you get on the plane, order yourself a glass of champagne. This is to celebrate the fact that you're even getting this far in the first place.

Your plane experiences some turbulence and has to make an emergency landing in Utah. You get off the plane and sit in the airport for a good twenty minutes before you fall asleep. You wake up a few hours later to discover that your plane has been boarding for a while and is set to leave at any minute. You frantically rush to the gate and are able to make it through at the last second. Pat yourself on the back and board your plane.

On arriving in Los Angeles, hail another taxi to your hotel. This time, the driver is another Rashid. Think to yourself, "could this be fate, or mere coincidence?" Arrive at the hotel as soon as possible. The bellhop runs to the taxi and grabs your bags out of the trunk. One of your bags pops open and all your clothes fall out. Sigh in disbelief as you put your clothes back in your bag. As the bellhop takes your bags to the elevator, check in at the front desk. The receptionist will give you the key to Room 409. You decide to take the stairs to stay in "Hollywood" shape and arrive at the fourth floor, where you notice the rooms are numbered starting with "2401." This is because Room 409 is on the twenty-seventh floor. Sigh hopelessly as you continue to climb the stairs. At the twenty-seventh floor, exit the stairwell and fall to the ground in exhaustion and agonizing pain. The elevator door opens and the bellhop steps out with your bags, headed for Room 409. Follow him to the end of the hall and greet him at the door to your room.

Once you've had a chance to relax, pull out your little black address book and start making calls to the friends you made from theater club. Realize that most of them haven't followed you to California, but went to New York instead, including both Amirs'. Shake your head and leave the hotel, this time using the elevator. Go to auditions, get rejected. Try to find an agent, get rejected. A manager? Rejected! Realize that rejection is part of the whole deal. You finally find a manager willing to accept you, but he requests thirty percent of your earnings. Reject him. After a long, grueling four months of rejection, you have saved up enough money somehow walking celebrity dogs with poor bowel control for a plane ticket home. As you walk back to your hotel to buy the ticket, get held up at gunpoint. The mugger runs off with your wallet, your identification, your hotel key and your cell phone. With no way to get back into the hotel room and no way to buy a ticket home or call for help, you decide to walk back to Michigan. Walk down the block, but watch your step for dog poop.

Private

I was sitting at my desk one day in my small corner office, when the phone started to ring. I was sure that my grump of a boss was calling, looking for something inane. He always found a way to get on my nerves, just about every time. Only today, I started to come down with hay fever, so a conversation with him would certainly make things "much better." Despite my best judgment, I swiped the phone off the receiver and put it up to my ear in a huff.

"Jon Daniels," I spouted my greeting. What can I say? For all I knew it could have been somebody else. It wasn't.

"Jon," my boss' voice came through in a drunken stupor, just like always, "I was s-speaking to yehr wife the other n-night, an' she tol' me sometin' juicy." I gasped in shock and astonishment. Surely, he was going on another one of his drunken rambles, where he would imagine that a conversation would have happened, when in reality it was babble between him and a cow in an open field. I had to be sure.

"Sir, I don't know what you're referring to," I replied hastily as I opened an instant message window to my wife. She was the kind of person who was into internet messages. I decided to learn it, just to appease her.

"Jon," my boss hiccupped into the phone, "Jon my boy, it's nothin' to be too embarrassed about, I just wanted to clear something up."

"Yes sir," I stated as I typed the following to my wife: *Honey, have you spoken to Mr. Jamerson lately?*

"Now, she told me something about something you'd done 'bout five y-years ago, at some p'rty." Her reply: *Yes, we had sort of a conversation yesterday.* Sort of a conversation, she says? If what my boss is saying is true, then it was more than just some sort of a conversation.

"Sir, whatever it was, it happened years ago. Surely it doesn't affect me as a person or an employee today." My response to my wife: *What did you tell him? He's talking to me about it right now, drunk as usual.*

"M'boy, I wan' you to go on an' guess what was said," he said, letting out another hiccup as my wife replied: *Are you seriously intimidated by that jackass?* Me, intimidated? No way!

"I don't think I could guess," I told him, "I don't think I could remember that far back." I frantically typed on my keyboard: *Seriously? No, I'm not. What did you tell him?*

"I wan' you to guess," he replied, and at that point I could swear that I smelled the pungent odor of whiskey seeping through the phone receiver, though I knew it was really my mind playing tricks on me. In the meantime, my wife had written back: *It's nothing embarrassing, I just told him about something sweet you had done while you were drunk.*

"Drunk?" I hadn't realized I said it out loud. I covered my mouth hastily, but before I could come up with a retort, my boss replied, "Ver' much, yessir."

I was starting to feel embarrassed, to say the least, and I didn't even know what had been discussed. I typed on my keyboard furiously: *Honey, please tell me what you told him, I'm starting to get very nervous.*

"So seriously, go 'head and guess," my boss said, followed by the loudest belch in the world. I swear, the smell of whiskey began to get stronger and stronger as the discussion, or rather, the interrogation continued. My wife responded: *Don't get nervous honey, it's not that big a deal. Nothing to be ashamed of or anything ;)*. If there's one thing I can't stand, it's those winking faces when I'm having tremors and pouring sweat from every orifice.

"Well, if I were to take a guess," I started, "I remember five years ago I struck it rich at Turning Stone," I said as my fingers trembled out the following on my keyboard: *He's driving me insane, you both are! He's not telling me and you're not telling me.*

"Tha's nah it," he replied, and then paused for what sounded like sipping a drink, "Tha's nah it at all. Why don' you guess it again." *Honey, relax...*

"Well, sir, I can't exactly recall." *Seriously, I feel like I'm having a heart attack.*

"Do yah wan' know what I know?" *OMG, honey, its fine.* How could she use internet lingo at a time like this? What if she shared with him one of my dirty little fantasies, or an embarrassing moment which I didn't remember because I was so drunk. My head started to feel heavy, I was sweating profusely, and every part of my body was shaking like a leaf. I had to get an answer now.

"What is it?" *TELL ME!!!!!*

"She tol' me 'bout when you serenaded her wit' Billy Joel, an' she tol' you 'bout how talented you were. Seriously, if you get that sc'red 'bout sometin' so sweet, you don' deserve a job here" *Well, I did tell him about when you serenaded me with Billy Joel, but u just yelled at me. I think we need to take a break...*

With that, my boss hung up and my wife logged off, and my head dropped onto my desk with a thud.

Recycled

None of us thought it was possible. It was certainly surreal to say the least. Two of our best friends, Joshua Stevens and Eleanor Hunter, two of the most opposite personalities you would ever meet, and here we were celebrating their ten year anniversary. Those two could not stand each other during our high school years. They would get into frequent arguments and heated debates over the silliest little things. I remember one year, they had the silliest little argument about the packaging of pudding, and the recyclability of said packages.

“You need to recycle those,” she would tell him as he tossed his pudding cup into the trash.

“What’s the point, it all goes to the same place anyway,” he said.

“That’s where you’re wrong. All that trash gets dumped into landfills and can cause pollution. At least if you recycle that, it can be reused.”

“Who would want to reuse a pudding cup I’ve already used?!”

“It’s not exactly like that…”

They went on like that for a few days afterward, neither party letting up ground in their argument. Yet, at the same time they felt it was those differences that attracted them to one another. Unlike most of the men I knew, Josh was always capable of compromise, and that was one of his strong suits. The only thing he needed to do was not despise his soul mate, and not be argumentative over her opinions. To the best of my recollection, the tour of the recycling plant we went on for Earth Science class may have changed his life for the better.

Eleanor was the person responsible for setting it up in the first place. She was the biggest environmentalist you would ever meet. Every weekend, she would pick up trash along the highway recycling every little plastic bottle and scrap of paper she could find. Yet at the same time, she was sick of Josh's arguing over recycling. Despite her many attempts to get him to toss a glass bottle into a recycle bin, he would continue to toss them into the trash. It was revenge time!

She convinced our science teacher to bring us to a recycling plant, to see what our recyclables went through. It is certainly the weirdest thing, how much that trip had changed him. We saw those Power Point slides of what happens to our trash when we don't recycle. We also saw the damage it could cause, if it all continued. Needless to say, nobody was more shocked, or appalled than Josh. When he proposed to Eleanor, he picked out a ring made of post recycled materials, and she was head over heels.

The years went by, and their marriage just got better and better. He became the manager of our local recycling plant, and every weekend he would host events for people to collect recyclables littered along roadsides and in parks. Just about anywhere there was litter; he was there to lead people to clean it up. His wife was so impressed, she made the compromise of going to the football games with him every Sunday, given he took his trash out with him to recycle it at home. She would usually fret about the fact that the stadium did not have any bins for recyclables, but that's practically because nobody cared about it as much as they did.

We applauded them, however, for sticking to the things that mattered the most to them. In most instances where people would give up on their dreams, because other people did not share their beliefs, they continued to go about their events every weekend. They continued to rally people to recycle, and I believe that is what made their marriage happy.

It wasn't until last week when I received their invitation in the mail. Pulling it out of the envelope, I noticed that it was shaped like that reduce, reuse and recycle triangle you find on just about everything nowadays. Josh had been my best friend since we were just young children, and I was not prepared to let him down on his anniversary.

Gift shopping for them was the easiest task in the world. I stopped by a local home improvement store and picked up a large recycle bin, and took it home to decorate it with glitter and pom-poms, and various other decorations made with post-recycled materials. Oh, the crazy things I did for that couple! I very much wanted them to find happiness for years to come, and what better way to start than with a brand new recycle bin?

I arrived at the celebration a little early, as I knew lugging this bin would be a chore and a half. Many other people had the same idea I had about arriving early. They were dressed up mainly in blue suits or green shirts, as a special way to celebrate the "marriage of recycling." It wasn't before long that the party got underway. As the guests seated themselves around tables with silk tablecloths and candles being held in recycled soda cans, Josh struck his champagne glass with his fork.

"I would like to propose a toast," he said, anxiously, almost like he had failed to rehearse what he planned to say. Of course, this was very much like Josh.

"I'd first like to propose this toast to everybody who came today. I want to thank you for your lovely gifts, though the best gift of all is the support you have had for us throughout the years. We have both made recycling a big part of our lives, yet at the same time, we were afraid that this fact would be dampened by lack of support. We are absolutely thrilled that all of our true friends are able to join us, not only today, but on the road that we call our lives, and that is most important of all."

This was followed by a round of cheering. Out of all the people there, I was cheering the loudest. I was very happy for Josh, I was happy for the fact that he found happiness in the place you would least expect. He raised his hands to silence the crowd. Almost immediately, everybody stopped clapping and cheering as Josh started to finish.

"Lastly, I'd like to propose this toast to my lovely wife. It's been ten amazing years, and I could not have found a happier time in my entire life. I know that when we were in school, we were usually at each other's throats, with our arguing over a lot of the little thing. However, those arguments helped me to open my eyes to the bigger picture. I learned that while a lot of the negatives of the world can't be solved so easily, nor may they ever be solved, sometimes it's the little things we do that can solve the biggest issues. I am thankful for you, darling, and for everything you've brought into my life. I'm hopeful for many more years of great joy and happiness"

With that, he planted a kiss on his wife's lips. Everybody raised their glasses, and began to drink as waiters and waitresses rolled out a grand banquet for the guests. At that moment, I did not care about the food. All I could do was stare at the happy couple, with a wide grin on my face, and think to myself how happy they were, and about how happy they would be, for the many years to come.

Host

Television is my life, or so it seems to me. I found my niche for performance when I was about eleven or so years old, when I tried out for a class play. The director was so impressed with my audition; I was given the lead role of Robin Hood, and after we had completed all the performances, was referred to a special school for the dramatic arts. It was a school filled with amazingly gifted children who had a knack for performing, just like I did.

What I found the most interest in, however, was comedy. I was the kind of guy who enjoyed making others laugh with my quick wit and my amazing jokes. I once got the toughest, meanest boy in my class to crack a smile, allowing me to keep my lunch money that day as he sauntered off. I personally thought of myself as a funnyman, or someone who was destined to bring joy to the world through my humor.

It wasn't long before I found my niche in Late Night Talk, and my desire to become a part of such a community grew exponentially. I enjoyed telling jokes, making people laugh, and performing. I felt like I could put on a good show, the kind of show that would make people tune in on a nightly basis. Conan O'Brian was my hero, in particular. He not only made his audience laugh with funny jokes and a quick wit, but he was also capable of putting on a good show. I wanted to model my abilities after what he was able to accomplish.

On reaching college, I decided right away to enroll in a dramatic arts program. It was there that I met and became close with my best friend, Mark. Mark was the kind of guy who would give the shirt off his back for the people he cared about. His path to college also followed a similar path to mine. He realized he had a gift at an early age, and was sent to a special school to build upon that gift, to make it grow, in a sense. Once he got to college, he found it to be a no brainer that he enroll in the dramatic arts program, one of the best in the nation.

After a while of getting to know each other, I finally decided to confide in him my dream of breaking into Late Night Talk Television, something that I had kept to myself for a long while.

"That actually sounds pretty cool," he said, "I think you're a pretty funny guy."

I breathed a heavy sigh of relief. We had only known each other for about a month at that point, and by my standards, that was not enough time to build the "friendship bias" that destroyed the very foundation of some great friendships.

"You really think so?" I replied, trying to remain as cool as possible.

"Of course," he replied, "I'm pretty impartial to Leno myself, but I think you'd be able to blow him out of the water."

"Well, I wouldn't say that, I'm really just trying to fine tune my craft, but I think that might be what I'd like to do."

"There's nothing wrong with having dreams. That's what we're all here for, is to have our dreams and to make them come true. I feel that our fate is totally up to us."

And with that, Mark offered his assistance in grooming me to become a top notch talk host. He told me that my best bet would be to start off as a stand-up comedian, and work my way from there. "A lot of the great talk show hosts started off as comedians," he assured me, "It not only helps you get comfortable in front of that kind of audience, but it also allows you to develop a style that you can call your own. Then, you go from there, simple."

Over the course of a few weekends, he'd take me to a low key comedy club in Downtown Manhattan. The place was very smoky, almost like one of those old time bars. We'd sit down around a creaky, wooden table on old chairs, anticipating the start of the show. As each comic took the stage, I would take down in-depth notes on their delivery, and their style, and sometimes even a joke that I had found especially funny.

It was one night after a trip to the comedy club that I had gotten the greatest proposition of my life. It was intermission, and Mark and I had decided to step outside for a cigarette. I personally try not to smoke heavily, as my parents were heavy smokers and I had seen what was becoming of them. I lit my cigarette and slowly began to drag on it a bit, when Mark decided to make conversation.

“So, do you have a routine yet?” He asked. I turned to look at him.

“Do I have a routine?”

“Yes,” he replied, “have you come up with any good jokes yet?”

“I guess it’s coming along,” was all I had to say.

“You guess?” He asked, “We’ve been coming here for a few weeks now, and that’s all you can say?”

That really was all that I could say. I had been extremely busy with my studies, that the last thing on my mind was the creation of a stand-up routine. Little did I know, a big burly man was listening in on our conversation. He walked up to us and extended his hand. Mark and I exchanged glances as he politely asked, “May I help you?”

“Ah, but indeed I can,” he said with a smile, “I’m John DeMarco, and I am the owner and proprietor of this comedy club, and I must say you’ve got quite an act going.” At first, we had thought he was being sarcastic. I did not feel as though there were anything funny about our exchange. However, he was more than serious.

"You seem to have such great chemistry together," he said, "If you can put something together, I'd love to have you both do a collaborative act."

This was something amazing. Mark and I were being invited to collaborate on a stand-up act of our very own. I could barely contain my excitement as Mr. DeMarco walked back into his club to prepare for after the intermission. Mark smiled at me as an affirmation, we would be doing this, and we would be in this together.

After the show, Mark and I approached Mr. DeMarco and agreed to his offer, and made arrangements for our performance. He agreed to give us three weeks to make any necessary preparations, and to come back raring and ready to go. I immediately rushed home, jumped on my computer, and began to frantically type up jokes that I was able to come up with instantaneously, in hopes of receiving Mark's approval. I had worked for approximately three or so hours, and had come up with a nice collection of jokes.

The next day, I brought them to class with me to show Mark, and he turned his nose up. "No way are these going to work," he said, "you need to think outside the box." Needless to say, I was disappointed by his remarks, but I realized that I needed to listen to the criticisms in order to come up with something fantastic. I returned home after class, hopped on my computer and deleted the original joke file. I set off to work, hoping I could come up with something much better.

It took me a longer time to come up with the jokes, and I wound up with less than before. I realized that I put as much thought as I could into each and every joke, every witty remark, was extremely well written in my eyes down to the last detail. I gave myself a nice pat on the back, excited about the job I did. When I showed them to Mark, however, he was not so pleased.

“Why is it you can’t write anything remotely funny?” He asked me. It was then that I realized that he had no interest in doing any writing at all.

“You could help me,” I replied to him.

“How? You always run home to work on it, you never ask for any feedback. Sometimes I feel like you want me to have no part in this.”

It was then that I noticed people start to gather around us, watching in anticipation our argument. Mark and I looked around at the people walking up and circling us. I wasn’t sure what was going on, but Mark had an idea. He nodded to me, and motioned for me to continue. I had not been more confused in my entire life, but I figured I wasn’t going to get anywhere with him unless I continued my rant.

“Sometimes I feel like you certainly don’t want to pull this off. I think you don’t really care about fame!”

“And sometimes I feel like you smell like a pig that’s rolled around in a nice mud bath. It certainly shows in your jokes, which stink!”

And with that, our audience began to chuckle. Mark nodded at me again, and all of a sudden I figured out exactly what was going on, or at least with him. He was improvising, and at the same time he was drawing a crowd and bringing smiles to their faces. It was also then which I realized that maybe I had been trying too hard with writing jokes. Mark motioned for me to continue again, and I decided to play along.

“I may smell like a muddy pig,” I said, “but I’m sure as heck going to cook your bacon!” I was certain that was as cheesy as it comes, but it still got me a positive reaction.

“Bacon? You’re the pig`! Don’t you mean you’re going to cook my goose?”

“Not yet, your goose still owes me about five grand.” Our audience roared in laughter. It was then that Mark outstretched his hand to me. I took his hand firmly and shook it. He helped me to realize that sometimes the funniest jokes come spur of the moment, and if we were going to get anywhere, we had to look down all avenues and figure out what worked best for us. Needless to say, Mark helped me find it.

~*~

On the night of our performance, we were both as cool and confident as ever. We pulled off the greatest, five minute fake argument anybody had ever seen, and the audience loved it. We were invited back to perform countless times, and so we did, each time growing better and better. It wasn’t before long when we were approached by a television producer, with a grand idea for a tag team Late Night talk duo. I’m very positive that it seemed to happen rather quickly, but who was I to judge? We had finally found our fame.

The Last Yard

"Jeremy, can you hear me? Please, wake up…"

The faint sound of a female voice was accompanied by vision so blurry, Jeremy Thompson could not make out what was happening. Almost instantly, the image faded to black, and the sounds around him began to get fainter. He was able to make out a few of the voices, and some of the words being spoken, although a majority of it was distorted to a point where it would almost be unrecognizable. Words and phrases such as "hard tackle" and "concussion" and "ambulance" haunted Jeremy's hearing and clouded his mind, which for the most part was absent of any activity. Whatever had happened to him, it was surely serious, as you typically don't hear words like that bunched so closely together in any other instance.

Jeremy Thompson was a football player for his high school, or rather, a football hopeful. He had played pee-wee football as a young child, and always dreamed of becoming a professional in the sport. Several of his coaches believed in him, and rightfully so. He had a gift that many children his age did not have without countless hours of hard work and dedication. At the age of seven, he once threw a football all the way down the local field, from one end zone to the other. His father just smiled, patted him on the head, and told him "someday, son, you'll make it." He continued to play, and easily made his high school football team, as a freshman with great hopes and even greater dreams.

Yet Jeremy's memory ended at the point where everything had become just a haze. And it would not be for another hour and a half before Jeremy awoke, with a groan, in a hospital bed. His mother and father, who had accompanied him, breathed heavy sighs of relief, his father shedding a tear. Jeremy groaned as he sat up in bed, lifting himself up and propping himself on some pillows.

"What happened?" he said, groaning in pain.

“You took a pretty hard hit,” his mother said, choking back tears, “we’re just glad you’re alright. Coach Conway will explain it to you.” With that, Coach Conway walked into the room. He was in his fifty’s, short and stout, with a whistle around his neck and a clipboard in his arms.

“Big Jenkins, he took you out good, but it’s good to see that you’re awake and aware,” said the coach, “how much do you remember?”

“Not a lot,” Jeremy said, still groaning, “I remember starting the game, and being down 19-13 with only a few seconds left in the game, and the football being passed to me, but that’s all I can really recall.”

“You caught it,” the coach replied frankly, and you were taken out hard, one yard from the end zone. Jenkins and the team were penalized, and we ended up winning, but in the end I feel we truly lost when you went down. It would have been your first High School touchdown, too.”

“Jenkins did this?” I asked somberly, “did he come?”

“He didn’t,” replied Coach Conway, “yet he seemed extremely distraught about the entire situation, I’m not sure it would have been a good idea for him to be here.” Jeremy only knew of Big Jenkins what he had seen of him, and he had seemed extremely serious about the game, and very mean at that. Jenkins was a short guy, probably a little shorter than Coach Conway. Yet, he was a bit on the round side. A lot of the kids in Jeremy’s school had questioned how he was able to play football and not tire out so quickly, yet the kids on the team did not worry about it. A lot of the kids who knew Jenkins personally said that, although he was serious about the game, he was really just a big teddy bear. This was all heresy to Jeremy, who was aware of the huge rivalry between the two schools, and that anything could be said to let your guard down about anybody.

It was at that moment, Jeremy's mother burst out into a fit of tears, his father walking over to comfort her. Jeremy mulled over everything that he had just heard. He could not believe everything he was hearing, partly because he could not truly remember it, and partly because he did not want it to be true.

"I want to go for a walk," Jeremy said, "I want to clear my head." Jeremy attempted to get out of the bed, but he struggled. He felt like he could not move his legs, yet he did not feel any pain, only slight numbness. Jeremy tried to move his legs again, but to no avail. Coach Conway gasped in shock as Jeremy's mother continued to sob. Jeremy's worst fears had been confirmed.

~*~

"Luckily, he only sustained a minor concussion, and he's very lucky for that," the doctor told Jeremy's parents and Coach Conway, "however, the hit he took caused him to sustain permanent damage to his spinal column. I'm afraid he's paralyzed from the waist down." Coach Conway put his head in his hands and shook it in disbelief. Jeremy's parents just looked on in shock. It appeared as if his mother just wanted to start crying again, letting out an overwhelming amount of emotion, but she just stood there, emotionless.

"What does this mean now?" his father asked, "you're saying our son may never walk again?"

"Though we always like to hold out hope for a different result, it is highly likely he'll never walk again." With this remark, the doctor walked past Jeremy's parents and into Jeremy's room.

"So, that's it?!" his mother asked in disbelief, "there's really nothing they can do about this?"

"This kind of injury," Coach Conway said, "there really is nothing they can do about. I'm really sorry." Jeremy's father began to express a bit of anger.

"That Jenkins," he said, "why didn't he come to check on our boy?"

"My guess is that he's just afraid of what Jeremy might say," Coach Conway said, "he seemed pretty upset about it as it is."

~*~

The next month was torture for Jeremy. He was placed in a wheelchair, and was finally able to go back to school within a couple of weeks. He had started to feel the effects of the concussion wear off, though he was still unable to walk. All he could think about was "why me?" As he rolled through the hallways of the school, several of the students patted him on the back, and told him things such as "he was brave," and "what courage this must take," and "I'm sorry to hear about your plight." Jeremy began to get frustrated. He did not want pity from his peers, nor did he want to hear about how courageous he was for going through these experiences. He just wanted to be left alone, to close himself off from the world. Although it was all in the student's best intentions, Jeremy felt that these best wishes were doing him more harm than good.

Around lunchtime, Jeremy wheeled himself up to the table where his best friend, Ken, sat. Jeremy and Ken had been friends since they were younger, though Ken didn't have much interest in football until Jeremy introduced him to it. Ken considered himself more of a computer geek, or even a math whiz, as he always immersed himself in programming languages and numbers. Ken's interest in football existed solely in the statistical aspect of it, especially after witnessing Jeremy's big hit.

"I'm glad to see you're back," Ken said, "I was worried you might have died or something!" Jeremy gave Ken a playful shove.

"Nope, I'm not dead yet," Jeremy exclaimed, "just not in the best of spirits."

"I understand, something like that must be tough."

"It's beyond tough. I've had people showing me remorse all this past month; it's really starting to get old." Jeremy unwrapped his turkey and mayo sub and took a huge bite out of it.

"I can see how something like that can be frustrating, yet you should realize it probably means that everybody cares about you."

"I don't know that they really care about me. All Conway would talk about was my 'gift' for football, and how I was finally going to bring a championship to this school. I just think they cared about my ability to play football," Jeremy took another bite out of his sandwich; "they'll probably just stop talking to me after a week." Ken just shrugged as he started to eat his lunch.

~*~

Coach Conway approached Jeremy in the hallway one day, after school had let out. Jeremy was closing up his locker after shoving yet another greeting card into the garglemesh of flowers, stuffed animals, and cards offering prayers and best wishes and hope for recovery and other mumbo jumbo that Jeremy could care less about.

"You know, you are still a big part of the team, it would mean a lot to us if you would sit on the sidelines to cheer us on," Coach Conway said, "we've got a big game against Middletown High coming up, and we'd like you to be a part of the festivities." Middletown High was the team Jeremy had played against when he took his life-changing hit. Surely, Jenkins would be there, not only to play but to taunt, though not a verbal taunt, but an emotional one. Jeremy could feel that by plainly watching Jenkins play, he would feel disgraced, almost like his entire world would come crashing down on him. It wasn't fair. Jeremy loved playing football, yet he couldn't do that anymore, while Jenkins could run around on a football field, play, laugh and have fun, all while showing no remorse for what happened.

Coach Conway had repeatedly told Jeremy that Jenkins had felt "absolutely horrible" about what happened and that he "wished it had never happened." Heresy, that's all it was to Jeremy, was heresy. He really wanted to hear it from Jenkins himself, but he never had. Coach Conway had always said that it was because he was afraid, though Jenkins was raised to believe that playing football involved never being afraid of anything. Jeremy had a hard time believing anything that the coach had told him, which led to his reluctance.

"I'll think about it," was all that could come from Jeremy's mouth.

~*~

The day of the big game came quicker than a speeding train, and there was a lot of commotion surrounding it. Students from both schools crowded the parking lot, bickering amongst themselves and each other, arguing over which team was better. They were wondering about whether the loss of the "great Jeremy Thompson" would affect their chances of winning, or if Jenkins had been given enough of a consequence to justify his crime. There were marching bands and cheerleaders, marching down the street to a triumphant tune, trying to raise the spirits of the people lost over the loss of their football messiah.

Jeremy and Ken just stayed across the street, watching it all. They stayed out of sight as best as they could, for Jeremy's sake, if anybody saw him, they would probably rush up to offer condolences or request an autograph. Jeremy shook his head in disbelief at the hubbub surrounding the event.

"It gets really crazy at these things," he said, "I never really got the chance to realize."

“It’s worse than usual,” Ken replied, “These people are here to celebrate you as they lambast Jenkins for taking you out the way he did.”

“I can’t say that I’m mad at Jenkins,” Jeremy said, clearly lying, “he was just playing the game.” Ken brushed off the white lie.

“Sometimes, people get more hyped up over a silly little game then they should,” Ken sighed. Jeremy thought about how true that statement was. He recalled a time in his youth when he went with his father to a Cowboy’s game. The Cowboy’s played their hearts out against their greatest rival, the New York Giants, and won a hard fought affair. After the game, he and his father witnessed the murder of a Cowboy fan at the hands of a Giants fan, just outside a bar near the stadium. Was that truly any way to react? Is an argument over a silly little game like football worth another person’s life?

Jeremy pondered those questions as he watched the opposing team getting off their bus. One by one, the players sauntered off the bus to a chorus of boos. The last person off the bus was Jenkins, a somber look on his face. He froze in fear in the middle of the road as the booing and the jeering grew louder and louder. He was clearly not pleased with what he had done, nor was he proud. He was also not pleased with the reaction of the fans. Jeremy caught this out of the corner of his eye, and he smiled. Jenkins really had remorse, yet Jenkins also knew that it was the game, and that day, Jeremy realized it too. Jenkins attempted to move from the middle of the road, but he felt just as paralyzed as Jeremy was. He knew he had a game to play, yet he also wanted to just get back on that bus and go home. His moral dilemma kept him frozen.

Jeremy caught a glimpse down the road, where a few rowdy fans climbed into a red pickup and started speeding down the road. Jenkins continued to stand there, in the middle of the road. He did not want to play, he did not want to cause harm, but he also couldn’t let his team down. Yet he was moments away from being severely harmed himself, possibly more than Jeremy. Jeremy wasn’t sure why he did what he did next, possibly because he kept thinking to himself “is this silly little game really worth a life?" Out of nowhere, a wheelchair sped out of the bushes across the street and slammed into Jenkins, toppling him onto the wheelchair and out of the road, as the pickup sped past. Jenkins barely had time to catch his breath before he was set onto the ground. Jeremy had saved his life. The crowd erupted into a roar. Jenkins shook Jeremy's hand out of sheer appreciation and bliss. Ken just looked on with a smile.

~*~

It was a few weeks later, and Jeremy was in better spirits. The other students had stopped showing him the pity he did not want, and instead were treating him as they would treat any other student. During lunch, he wheeled up to the table where Ken was sitting, an envelope sitting right in front of him.

"I saw Jenkins," he said, looking up at Jeremy.

"Did you?" Jeremy asked. Ken nodded, picking up the envelope.

"He wasn't sure when he was going to see you again, so I agreed to give you this card from him," Ken said, expecting a rolling of the eyes from Jeremy, or the usual reaction. Instead, Jeremy took the card joyously from Ken.

"Thank you," he said, wheeling away toward his locker. Jeremy opened the envelope to find the greeting card. He opened it up to read it. *Jeremy, I'm very sorry about what I did to you. I felt absolutely horrible about it for a long time, but I'm glad you showed me that it's just a game, and that you don't hate me for it. I hope you feel better soon. Signed, Jenkins.*

Unlike the other cards, which he just stuffed away in his locker, Jeremy pulled some tape from his backpack and proudly taped the card to the front of his locker. He knew that he would never be able to walk again, but at least now he'd be able to smile about it.

www.ingramcontent.com/pod-product-compliance
Ingram Content Group UK Ltd.
Pitfield, Milton Keynes, MK11 3LW, UK
UKHW041832200726
13854UKWH00003BA/1110